HOW TO CROSS THE ROAD
AND NOT TURN INTO A PIZZA

Other books by Anne Fine include:

ANNE FINE

Illustrated by Tony Ross

WALKER BOOKS
AND SUBSIDIARIES

LONDON • BOSTON • SYDNEY

First published 2002 by Walker Books Ltd
87 Vauxhall Walk, London SE11 5HJ

This edition published 2002

2 4 6 8 10 9 7 5 3 1

Text © 2002 Anne Fine
Illustrations © 2002 Tony Ross

The right of Anne Fine to be identified as author
of this work has been asserted by her in accordance
with the Copyright, Designs and Patents Act 1988

This book has been typeset in Monotype Baskerville and Soupbone Bold

Printed and bound in Great Britain by
The Guernsey Press Co. Ltd

British Library Cataloguing in Publication Data:
a catalogue record for this book is
available from the British Library

ISBN 0-7445-9034-5

For Jack and Toby Warren

LUCKY

On Monday, when Miss Talentino
came into class, everyone was
whispering.

"Did you hear about Tom's
brother?"

"No, not his brother. His *cousin*."

"Harry."

"No. *Larry*."

"At the big school."

"Not the big school. The *middle*
school."

"He was crossing the road."

"No. Taking a short cut over the roundabout."

"No. Fetching his ball."

"And along came this giant great lorry."

"No, no. A yellow *car*."

"A *motorbike*."

"Anyway, he's in hospital."

"Broken both arms."

"No. *Legs*."

"And so he gets better properly, he has to be strapped down so he can't even *move*."

"For six whole weeks."

"No. Four."

"Four at the *most*."

"But then he'll have to wear a sort of corset thing for six more weeks."

"One of those scratchy, itchy things."

"All summer."

"*And* he'll miss Sports Day."

"And playing the drums in the concert."

"And the camping trip."

"He'll miss his friends, too. Except for the ones who live close enough to visit."

"And he was *lucky*."

"Yes. Lucky!"

"Yes. He was *lucky*."

"Yes," said Miss Talentino, who'd been listening. "He was *lucky*." She thought for a moment, and then she asked, "Who, out of all the people in this class, is allowed to cross roads yet?"

Everyone put their hand up.

"By themselves," she said.

Everyone put their hand down, except for Simon, who wasn't listening properly because he was looking ahead in the maths book.

"I said '*by themselves*'," she repeated.
Simon's hand came down as well.

"I *would*," said Jason, "except my
mum always says: 'Not this year,
maybe next year'."

"And *I* would," said Herbert,
"except that I'm not allowed yet."

"I would," said Melissa, "*except* I'm
always with my mum and brother,
and my brother's too young to cross
roads."

"And I *might*," said Felicia, "because my mum and dad said maybe, when it gets to my birthday." She scowled horribly. "But then again, they said that last year, and they didn't let me."

"Mmmm," said Miss Talentino. "Interesting. Very interesting..."

Then she turned to write the date on the board. "Shall we get started?"

FLAT TROUBLE

Next morning, as soon as the lollipop lady had gone home for coffee, Miss Talentino told them all, "Put your jackets back on again, because I'm taking you out in the playground."

"I don't want to go," said Simon. "Not if we're missing maths. Maths is the only thing I'm any good at, and it's not fair if we miss the only thing I'm any good at by going out to play early."

"We're not going out to play," said Miss Talentino. "We're going to do something special."

She led them into the playground
and then went out through the gates
and stood on the pavement while
they peered at her through the school
fence like monkeys.

"This isn't maths," Simon grumbled loudly.

"Try and be patient," said Miss Talentino, and looked out at the road in front of her.

"Should I cross now?" she asked, as the traffic whizzed past her.

"No!" everyone shouted, except for Simon, who was feeling grumpy.

And even he said "Yes" quietly, so she could hardly hear it, because he was trying to be patient.

Miss Talentino waited till the road was as empty as a desert the day after one lonely camel has passed by.

"Should I cross now?"

"Yes!" shouted everyone, except for Sadie, who was cautious by nature. And even she said, "*May*be..."

"My mum says 'maybe' is no good," said Felicia. "Not when you're crossing roads. You can end up in big trouble with 'maybe'."

"Flat trouble," Arif giggled. "Look!"

He pointed. Out in the middle of the road there was a squashed round patch with little tufty bits sticking out at the edges.

"Bad luck," said Helena.

"Prickly pizza!" said Arif.

And they all stared at the hedgehog that had crossed on a maybe.

"That could be me," said Simon gloomily. "I'm useless at practically everything except maths, so I'll be useless at road-crossing, just as soon as anyone lets me." He scowled at Miss Talentino through the holes in the wire fence and added, "Which is why I'd much rather be back in the classroom doing maths, like we're supposed to, than out here staring at squashed hedgehogs."

But because she'd said "Try and be patient", he added it very, very quietly.

REAL AND PRETEND

Miss Talentino said, "Can you all see me?" and "Are you all listening?" as usual, and then she asked them: "When our class did our little play in the school Christmas show, did we use a real snowman?"

"No," chirruped everyone.

"And when we did our display of 'How the Planets Move' on the sports field on Open Day, did we use real stars and the real moon?"

"No."

"And when we did 'Dinosaurs and How They Lived' for a special class project, did we use a real velociraptor?"

"No."

"Right," said Miss Talentino. "And this morning, to save you all from turning into pizzas, we're not going to use the real road. We're going to use a pretend one. Who has a stop-watch I can borrow?"

Amber got hers off her wrist first, and handed it through a hole in the fence.

Miss Talentino took it. "Now," she said, "I'm going to cross the road. Not running. Not dawdling. Just walking sensibly and briskly."

She timed herself, and everyone whose watch could time things timed her too.

"I counted five and a half seconds," called Miss Talentino from the other side.

"Six," said Surina.

"No time at all," said Callum, who hadn't managed to get his stop-watch bit started.

"Five seconds exactly," said Simon.

And because, in the classroom, he was so good at maths, they agreed they would take it as five seconds exactly.

Miss Talentino waited for a gap in the traffic, then crossed the road back again.

"Six and a bit," said Surina.

"Eighteen," said Callum, but this time he hadn't been able to make his stop-watch bit stop.

Miss Talentino ignored both of them and stuck with Simon's five seconds.

Then she called Josh out onto the pavement and stood him with his back against the fence.

Bethany and Georgia began tickling his ears through the little holes.

"Stop that," Miss Talentino told them. "This is important."

"Not as important as maths," grumbled Simon. But because he was still trying to be patient, he grumbled it quietly so she wouldn't hear.

"Now," Miss Talentino told Josh, "walk from the fence to the safety barrier."

"It's two steps!" Simon told her.

Miss Talentino ignored him. Instead she warned everyone, "Stopwatches ready?"

They all got set.

Josh went from the fence to the barrier in two steps.

"See?" Simon told her.

Miss Talentino still ignored him. "How long did it take?" she asked the air around her.

"No time at all," said Callum, who hadn't had time to press his little button.

"Half a second," said Sadie.

"Three quarters," said Simon because, as well as complaining, he'd been using his stop-watch properly.

Miss Talentino said to Josh, "Do it again. But this time try and take a whole five seconds."

"How?"

"Shuffle."

So, this time, Josh shuffled.

"Six and a quarter seconds," said Simon. "Too long. Try again, taking tiny steps."

Josh stuck out his arms and took silly mincing-princess steps.

"Eight seconds," Simon told him. "Faster please."

This time Josh took tiny steps, but left out the silly mincing.

"Five seconds!" Simon said. "Perfect!"

"Exactly the time it takes to cross the real road," Miss Talentino reminded them. Then she sent Josh to stand with his back touching the fence again.

"Right," she said. "Cross your pretend pavement road when you think it would be safe to cross the real one."

Josh watched the traffic flashing by.

Cars came past fast in one direction. Cars came by fast in the other. Two huge and noisy lorries rumbled by. Then a man on a bike cycled past. Then another lorry swept by.

"It looks a bit different without the lollipop lady," said Josh.

"Doesn't it just!" said Miss Talentino.

FEELING A BIT TREMBLY

Josh had a think.

"Now?" he asked.

"I'm not saying anything," said Miss Talentino. "You're on your own here."

Everyone pressed their nose tighter against the fence and waited to see if Josh would make a terrible mistake like Tom's cousin Larry.

And end up as pretend pizza.

Josh took a giant breath. "Now!"
he said, and started his little shuffle
steps. It took him exactly five seconds
to cross his pretend road and get to
the safety barrier.

Nothing whooshed past in front of
him on the real road. But, just as he
put his fingers on the safety barrier, a
lorry went hurtling past.

"Phew!" Josh said. "That was a bit close."

And he looked at the hedgehog that went on a maybe.

"Fancy another go?" asked Miss Talentino.

"Not really," said Josh, "I feel a little bit trembly. Let someone else have a turn."

"Me!" shouted Felicia.

So Josh went back in the playground, behind the fence, and Felicia came out onto the pavement. She practised the tiny little shuffle steps until she'd got them about right. Then she leaned back against the fence.

Helena tickled her ear through one of the little holes.

"Don't distract me," said Felicia. "I'm thinking."

She watched the traffic. It was horrible. It went on for ever and ever. Each time she thought she saw a little space, something came along to spoil it.

And some things came along very fast.

"Hurry up," said Anthea. "I want to get to my turn."

"No," Sadie insisted. "Better safe than sorry. You mustn't hurry, Felicia. My dad says it takes as long as it takes, and sometimes it takes ages."

"That's right," said Bethany. "And my grandpa says it's much, much better to be five minutes late in this world than seventy years early in the next."

"More than five *minutes* late," grumbled Anthea. "More like five *years!*"

"Shhh!" everyone scolded, and looked at Miss Talentino, expecting her to tell Anthea off for rushing Felicia when it was something so important. But Miss Talentino just stared at the clouds over her head as if she hadn't been listening.

Finally, *finally*, just as they'd all practically grown beards down to their feet, Felicia took her tiny steps across the pavement to the safety barrier.

And nothing passed on the real road while she was doing it.

"Yes!" Felicia said, punching the air in triumph. "I would have got over safely!"

"My turn!" said Anthea.

She crossed the pretend road and then, as soon as she reached the barrier, looked back over her shoulder and crossed it back again.

"Show-off!" said everyone.

"You got an easy patch," said Geoffrey.

"No bickering, please," said Miss Talentino. "Try and be grateful she's alive. Terence! Your turn."

Terence was good at it too. So was Melissa. And, one by one, Miss Talentino called out everyone in the class.

Then she reached Simon.

MATHS AND VELOCIRAPTORS

Simon came out and stood on the pavement with his back to the fence.

"Good thing it's not the real road I'm going to try and cross," he said gloomily. "I'd probably end up like that hedgehog."

And he stared at the prickly pizza on the tarmac.

"You know your trouble?" said Miss Talentino. "You think you're only good at maths. But what you don't realize is that maths sneaks its way into practically everything. Even into this."

"Crossing the road?"

Miss Talentino sighed. "Who did the counting to see how long it took to cross?"

"Me," Simon said. "And Callum and Surina. Oh, and you."

"And did we all get the same answer?"

"No."

"And whose answer did we choose?"

"Mine," Simon said.

"Right again," said Miss Talentino.

"And since you're well on top so far, we'll do a tiny bit of maths from the book for people older than you. As you will notice, some things on the real road come zipping by fast, and some things come ambling past slowly, and most come rumbling by in between. All different speeds. But in the big maths book they're all called" – she took a big fancy breath and spread her arms – *"velocity."*

"Velocity?"

"Velocity. It's the maths word for speed."

Simon said it again, to remember it. "Velocity." Then he remembered something else. "Velociraptor!" He grinned. "The dinosaur that gets you quick!"

"Not half," said Miss Talentino. "And since you're still keeping up, you might as well know that some of these things on the road come down it one way and some of them come down the other. But, in the big maths books, whichever way they come is called their" – she took another big fancy breath and said it loud and clear – *"line of approach."*

"Line of approach?"

"Line of approach."

Miss Talentino pointed up in the air. "And, since we are doing a bit of extended work here, and you are doing so well, I may as well mention that if a really bad-tempered seagull happened to decide to divebomb you at exactly the same time as you were standing here trying to work out if it was safe to cross, it would be coming at you at what is called its *angle of approach* as well."

"Wouldn't it just!" said Simon, imagining a furious bird swooping out of the air directly at him, straight and steep.

Miss Talentino patted his shoulder. "So try and think of it as a question in one of the tests in our maths book." She sighed. "And try very hard to get it right, so you don't end up as a pizza, like that hedgehog."

Simon stood with his back to the fence and watched the traffic. Looked at in one way, it was a big noisy confusing mess. But looked at like a question in the maths book, he knew that he could have a go at it. He watched to see what was coming, and from where, and how fast. Three times he didn't go, even though he was almost totally sure it was all right, and knew afterwards that he could have.

And then – at last – he went across the pretend road.

Five seconds exactly: shuffle, shuffle, shuffle, until he reached the safety barrier.

And, on the real road, nothing passed that would have splatted him.

Miss Talentino led everyone back
to the classroom.

"Can we go home and say we know how to cross roads by ourselves now?" asked Terence.

Miss Talentino grinned. "If you went home and said that you could do dividing perfectly because you'd got one easy sum right, do you think they'd believe you?"

"Probably not," said Terence.

Felicia groaned. "I bet my parents are like you. I bet they make me do it hundreds of times before they admit I know it properly."

"Thousands!" agreed Jason.

"Millions!" said Helena.

"Billions!" said Herbert.

"Trillions!" said Anthea.

"Frillions!" said Arif.

"There's no such things as frillions," Simon told them.

And because he was good at maths –
as well as practising crossing busy
roads – they believed him.

ANNE FINE

Anne Fine was elected to take on the prestigious position of Children's Laureate in 2001. A highly acclaimed author, she has won the Smarties Book Prize, the Guardian Children's Fiction Award and, on two occasions, the Carnegie Medal and the Whitbread Children's Book Award, most recently for *The Tulip Touch*. She was also voted Children's Author of the Year in 1990 and 1993. Her book *Goggle-eyes* was dramatized as a BBC TV serial and *Madame Doubtfire* was turned into the hugely successful Hollywood film, *Mrs Doubtfire*. She has two daughters and lives in County Durham.

You can find out more about Anne Fine and her books by visiting her website: www.annefine.co.uk